Padma Shri Pran

Maurice Horn, the editor of World Encyclopedia of Comics, has described cartoonist PRAN as Walt Disney of India.

Entertaining generation after generation, his comics have been constant companion of all the growing youngsters providing fun and amusement through his famous characters like CHACHA CHAUDHARY, SABU, SHRIMATIJI, PINKI, BILLOO, RAMAN etc. More than 600 of his titles are selling well in the market, and numerous comic strips are regularly appearing in various newspapers. His CHACHA CHAUDHARY comics had already been adapted for a TV Serial, and ran continuously for 600 episodes on a premier channel.

Travelling widely over the globe, he delivers lectures at various International Conferences. He has also been honoured with 'People of The Year Award' by Limca Book of Records for popularizing comics. His comic book 'United We Stand' was released in 1983 by the then Prime Minister Mrs. Indira Gandhi, and is still very popular among children.

Publisher

BILLOO
FISHING

I CAUGHT ONE !
I TOO !
WHAT IS BILLOO'S SITUATION ?
I GOT THIS SHOE.
THIS USELESS CAP.

I CAUGHT ANOTHER FISH.
NOW WHAT DID I GET ?
USELESS HANDBAG.
OH ! IT HAS DIAMONDS.
www.chachachaudhary.com

DIAMONDS !
THEY'RE VERY PRECIOUS !
WE SHOULD INFORM THE POLICE
I'LL CALL THE POLICE
IT'S NOT REQUIRED.
THESE DIAMONDS ARE MINE ! I THREW THEM IN THE RIVER TO ESCAPE FROM THE POLICE.

HAND THEM OVER TO ME.
IF YOU TRY TO BE CLEVER, I'LL SHOOT.
ALL OF YOU VACATE THIS PLACE.
COME.

OH ! MY PISTOL !
YOU CAUGHT HIM WONDERFULLY !
GRR
RR !
I WON'T SPARE YOU.
© PRAN'S FEATURES

FIRST THINK OF YOURSELF.
OUCH !
AHH !
NOW REMAIN LIKE THIS TILL THE POLICE COME.
AHHH !
WELL DONE, BILLOO ! THANKS FOR HELPING US. OFFICERS! NAB HIM WITH THE STOLEN DIAMONDS.
COME TO THE POLICE STATION TO COLLECT YOUR REWARD.

BiLLOO
HILL STATION
IT'S A WONDERFUL PLACE!

VALLEY SPREAD FAR AND WIDE...
www.chachachaudhary.com

THERE'S NOTHING TO MATCH THE SNOW-CAPPED MOUNTAINS.

IT WILL BE GREAT IF GOD SHOWERS A LITTLE CREAM ALSO.
HOW COME ?
THERE'S ICE SPREAD ALL AROUND. MIX IT WITH CREAM. IT'LL BECOME ICE-CREAM.
RIGHT.
BUT SNOW CAN BE ENJOYED LIKE THIS ALSO.

I'LL MAKE A SNOW BOY.
I'LL THROW AN ICE BOMB.
I'LL DO SKIING.

YAY !!!
RIDING ON THE ROPEWAY AFTER COMING TO A HILL STATION IS NECESSARY.
HEY!!

HEY, BILLOO!
HI, JOJI!
SUDDENLY
OH!
WHAT'S THIS?
WHY HAS THE TROLLEY STOPPED?
© PRAN'S FEATURES

THERE'S A PROBLEM WITH THE ROPEWAY.
SOMETHING'S GOT STUCK IN THE ROUTE OF THE ROPEWAY, NEED TO CALL A CRANE TO REMOVE IT.
CRANE WILL TAKE A LOT OF TIME IN REACHING HERE.
WHAT WILL HAPPEN TO THE PASSENGERS STUCK TILL THEN ?
SORRY ! THERE'S NO OTHER OPTION.

BILLOO ! WE'RE STUCK HERE. DO SOMETHING.
I AM SCARED.
SOMEBODY SAVE US.
THERE'S SOME PROBLEM IN THE ROPEWAY ROUTE.
I'LL DO SOMETHING TO REACH THERE.

BILLOO IS SKIING AT HIGH SPEED AND MOVES TOWARDS SLIDE POINT.
YAY !!
I HOPE THE STICK HITS AT THE RIGHT POINT.
HITTT !
GRRRR !

TROLLEY STARTS MOVING.
THANK YOU, BILLOO !
BILLOO, SAVED US.
ENJOY.
SNEEZE !!
SNIFF ! SNIFF !
SO MANY BENEFITS OF A HILL STATION BUT ONE UNAVOIDABLE DRAWBACK.

PRAN'S
CHACHA CHAUDHARY
AND
SWACHH BHARAT

CHACHA CHAUDHARY AND SWACHH BHARAT

GEETA, YOU ALSO JOIN US.
MUMMY, I AM ALSO GOING.
CAN I PLAY WITH YOUR TOY?
OF COURSE!
KIDS, DON'T MAKE ANY NOISE.
WHERE ARE WE GOING?
TO GULZAR GARDEN.

HOW FAR IS IT ?
IT'LL TAKE HALF AN HOUR.
WOW ! WHAT A PLACE.
EVERYONE GET YOUR BAGS AND COME HERE.
MANU, LET'S PLAY FOOTBALL.
COME !

CHACHA JI, NOW IT'S TIME FOR LUNCH.
COME ON KIDS, LET'S HAVE LUNCH.
CHACHA JI, THESE KIDS HAVE LITTERED THE WHOLE PLACE.

THAT'S VERY BAD.
WHY DON'T YOU PUNISH THEM ?
NOT PUNISHMENT, BUT A LESSON.
MANU ! YOU ARE ALWAYS RIGHT. IT'S A BAD HABIT.
WHO HAS PUT THIS GARBAGE IN THE DUGDUG?
LOOK CAREFULLY. IT'S THE SAME GARBAGE WHICH YOU HAD LEFT IN THE PARK.

UFF !!
WE SHOULD HAVE DONE IT BEFORE.
YOU HAVE DIRTIED THE WHOLE PLACE.
WE SHOULD TAKE CARE OF THIS.
NOW, THEY WILL NOT LITTER ANY PLACE IN FUTURE.
COME ON KIDS, PUT THE WASTE PAPER, BOTTLES AND FOOD IN DIFFERENT COLORED BINS.

I'LL TAKE YOU TO A PLACE WHERE THIS GARBAGE IS RECYCLED THROUGH MACHINE.
WHERE CHACHA JI ?
EVERYBODY JUMP INTO DUGDUG.
PINKI, TALK LATER, FIRST COME INTO DUGDUG.
BHARAT, SHOW THEM HOW YOU RECYCLE THE GARBAGE INTO MANURE WITH THE HELP OF MACHINE.
PUT THE GARBAGE IN THE MACHINE AND START IT.
SEE, IT IS CONVERTED INTO MANURE. IT'S VERY USEFUL.

IT IS A PART OF SWACHH BHARAT ABHIYAN UNDER MINISTRY OF URBAN DEVELOPMENT.
NEVER THROW THE WASTE. USE IT IN SOME MANNER. THERE WON'T BE ANY DISEASE SPREADING AROUND.
WE'LL HAVE DOUBLE BENEFIT.
THAT'S DOUBLE USEFUL. SWACHH BHARAT ABHIYAN CAN ONLY BE SUCCESSFUL WHEN WE ALL WILL KEEP OUR AREA CLEAN.
WE ALL NEED YOUR COOPERATION.
YOU SHOULD TAKE A PLEDGE TO KEEP CLEANLINESS AROUND YOU.
WE SWACHHA GRAHI FAMILY PLEDGE TO KEEP OUR SURROUNDINGS CLEAN.

स्वच्छ भारत
एक कदम स्वच्छता की ओर
सत्यमेव जयते
Ministry of Urban Development
Government of India
कम्पोस्ट अपनाओ,
फार्म हाउस में हरियाली लाओ.
• फार्म हाउस में कम्पोस्ट का इस्तेमाल कीजिए
• ये मिट्टी को उपजाऊ बनाती है
• इसे आप नज़दीकी फर्टिलाइज़र की दुकान से खरीद सकते हैं
अधिक जानकारी के लिए
1969

BILLOO
MAGIC CARPET
GOD KNOWS SINCE WHEN THIS CARPET HAS BEEN LYING IN THIS DUNGEON LIKE STORE ROOM !!
WE NEED TO THROW IT WITH THE OTHER JUNK.
OH !!

WHAT'S FALLEN FROM THE CARPET ?
IT IS A FLYING CARPET. ITS MAGIC POWERS WILL FINISH SOON.
MAGIC CARPET !!
HURRAH !!
NO NEED TO WASTE TIME. IT'S A MAGIC CARPET !
COME LET'S ENJOY THE FLIGHT.

LET'S MOVE!
HMMM!
JOJI!
BILLOO, THAT'S YOU?
YES! THIS IS OUR MAGIC CARPET. YOU ALSO COME.
www.chachachaudhary.com

YAY !!
LOOK
THERE.
BILLOO'S GOT A
FLYING CARPET.
TAKE OUT
YOUR STICKS,
MY BOYS.
THAT CARPET
SHOULD BE
MINE.
COME !

THIS MAGIC CARPET IS THE BEST SOLUTION TO THE TRAFFIC IN THIS CITY.
YOU'RE RIGHT.
OH!
FIRE ! FIRE !!

THAT CHILD IS STUCK UP ON THE TERRACE.
NO ONE IS ABLE TO REACH HIM DUE TO THE FIRE.
WE CAN REACH THERE.
COME!
THANKS!

WELL DONE!
NOW LET'S ROAM AROUND AGAIN.
STOP!
DON'T FLY AWAY NOW. ELSE YOU WON'T BE SPARED.
OH! BAJRANGI AND THE OTHER WRESTLERS!
© PRAN'S FEATURES

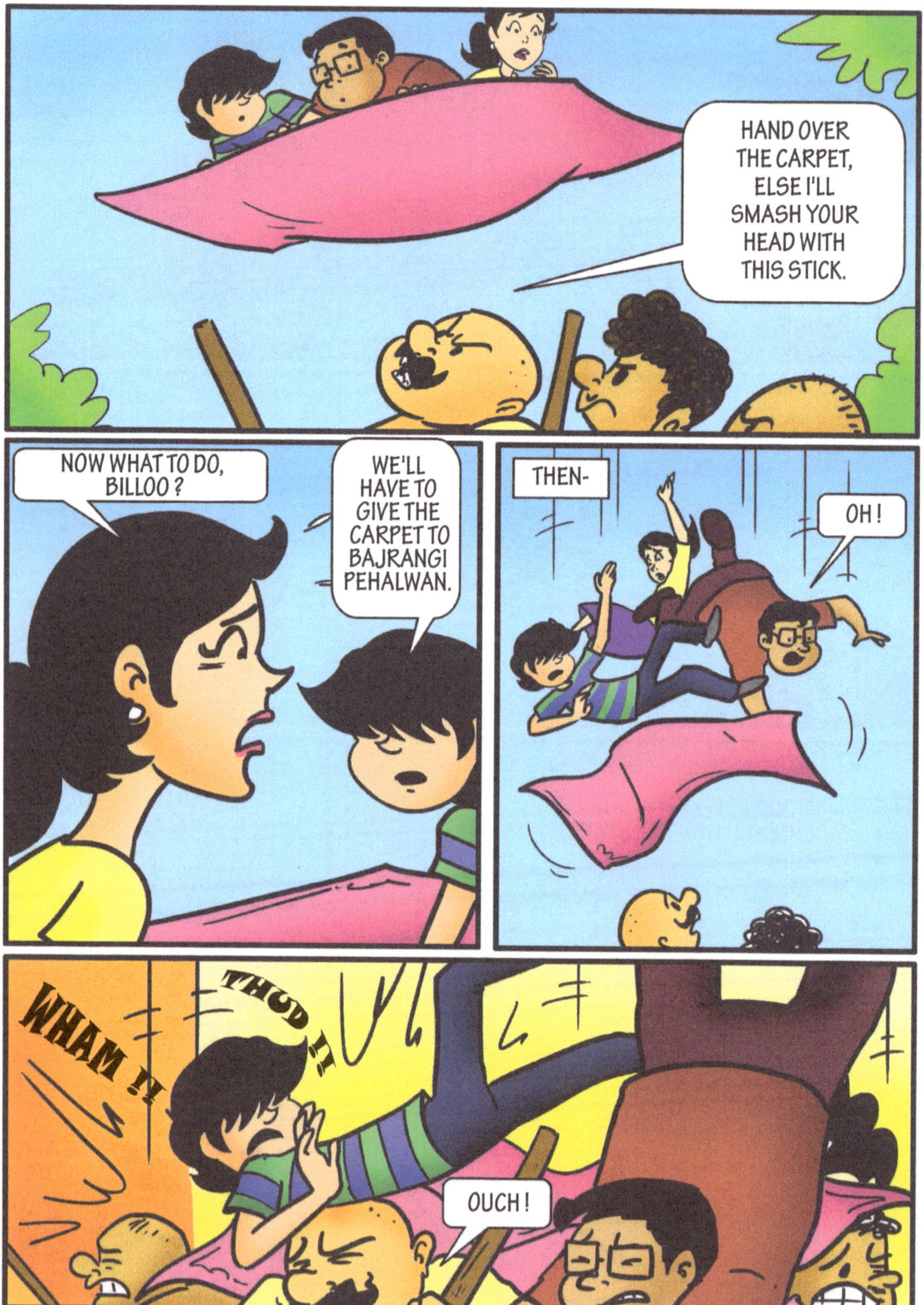
HAND OVER THE CARPET, ELSE I'LL SMASH YOUR HEAD WITH THIS STICK.
NOW WHAT TO DO, BILLOO ?
WE'LL HAVE TO GIVE THE CARPET TO BAJRANGI PEHALWAN.
THEN-
OH !
WHAM !!
THUD !!
OUCH !

OH!
AHH!!
YOU WANTED THE CARPET, TAKE IT.
BY THE WAY NOW THIS CARPET IS NOT MORE THAN RUBBISH
AS ITS MAGIC POWER IS FINISHED.

BILLOO
POLE HIGH JUMP
THERE'S A POLE VAULT HIGH JUMP COMPETITION IN SCHOOL.
NEED TO PRACTICE A LITTLE.
HEY, BILLOO !
HEY JOJI !
www.chachachaudhary.com

MEET MY COUSIN, RABADU.
HELLO!
HELLO!
WHAT'S GOING ON?
PRACTICE OF POLE VAULT JUMP.

GOOD ! SHOW IT TO ME.
OK.
OH, WAITTT !!
OH !!
AHH !! WHY DID YOU STOP ME ?

YOU'RE HOLDING THE POLE WRONGLY.
HOLD IT PROPERLY AND START AGAIN.
NOW IT'S FINE.
WAIT!
NOW WHAT HAPPENED?
NOW YOU'RE NOT RUNNING PROPERLY.
© PRAN'S FEATURES

SEEMS YOU KNOW A LOT ABOUT POLE VAULT.
YOU'RE RIGHT.
I THINK YOU SHOULD DO IT AND SHOW ME.
AS YOU WISH.
JUMP ACROSS THIS WALL.
LOOK ON.

NOW I CAN PRACTICE PROPERLY BECAUSE...
RABADU'S CAUGHT IN WET MUD. IT WILL TAKE A LONG TIME FOR HIM TO ...
COME OUT.

BILLOO
SUMO'S FOOD
MOTI ! YOU'VE SPOILED MY BED. GET UP !
HEARD OR NOT ?
ATTRACT HIM WITH A PASTRY. HE'LL COME RUNNING.
HERE, TAKE A PASTRY.

ENJOY IT IN THE OPEN AIR.
SWISHHHH !!
OH ! THAT BIRD FLEW AWAY WITH MOTI'S PASTRY.

I'LL TEACH YOU A LESSON.
CHILD ! THE BIRD IS SITTING HIGH UP ON THE TREE.
HOW'LL YOU TEACH IT A LESSON?
I HAVE ANOTHER PASTRY. YOU CAN TAKE THAT.
BOW ! WOW !!
I'LL KEEP IT HERE.
www.chachachaudhary.com

SWISHHHH !!
WHAM !
CRACK !
HO ! HO !!
HA ! HA !! ITS BEAK HAS BROKEN. I HAD HIDDEN A STONE IN THE PASTRY.
MOTI ! WHY'RE YOU SAD ? OH YES ! YOU'RE HUNGRY.
COME, LET'S HUNT FOR FOOD.
© PRAN'S FEATURES

SUMO! WHY DO YOU EAT SO MUCH?
I WON'T BE HEALTHY, IF I DON'T EAT ENOUGH.
WHAT IS YOUR PROBLEM, COOK?
I FEEL VERY TIRED COOKING SO MANY CHAPATIS.
HO! HO!! I'LL EAT ALL THIS.
?!
!!
OH! HE'S TAKING MY CHAPATIS.
YOU'VE PROVOKED SUMO!!

I'LL SEND YOU TO HELL.
CRACK K !
THUD D !
AAOOW !
LET ME HAVE THE REST OF THE CHAPATIS.
OHH !! MY FOOD !!

Diamond TOONS
Largest selling comics in India
PRAN'S CHACHA CHAUDHARY AND SWACHH BHARAT
₹ 50 48P
Largest selling comics in India
PRAN'S BILLOO AND FISHING
₹ 50 48P
Largest selling comics in India
PRAN'S PINKI REAL WATCHMAN
₹ 50 48P
Availabe in Hindi, English, Marathi, Gujarati & Bangla
Chacha Chaudhary, Billoo & Pinki comics also available in Digest.
PRAN'S CHACHA CHAUDHARY DIGEST - 1
₹ 100 96P Size: 6.5"X9"
PRAN'S CHACHA CHAUDHARY DIGEST - 2
₹ 100 96P Size: 6.5"X9"
PRAN'S CHACHA CHAUDHARY DIGEST - 3
₹ 100 96P Size: 6.5"X9"
PRAN'S CHACHA CHAUDHARY DIGEST-4
₹ 100 96P Size: 6.5"X
PRAN'S BILLOO'S DIGEST - 1
₹ 100 96P Size: 6.5"X9"
PRAN'S BILLOO'S DIGEST - 2
₹ 100 96P Size: 6.5"X9"
PRAN'S PINKI DIGEST - 1
₹ 100 96P Size: 6.5"X9"
PRAN'S PINKI DIGEST - 2
₹ 100 96P Size: 6.5"X
Diamond TOONS
X-30, Okhla Industrial Area Phase-II, New Delhi-110020, India
Tel.: 011-40712100, 40712200 Email: sales@dpb.in